WHEN IT SNOWS

RICHARD COLLINGRIDGE

FEIWEL AND FRIENDS

NEW YORK

When it snows...

all the cars are stuck and
the train disappears.

So, I follow the footprints

until I find a new way
to get around.

I play for the rest of the way

to the place where
the snowmen live.

And when the sun sinks,
I follow a bright light into the dark.

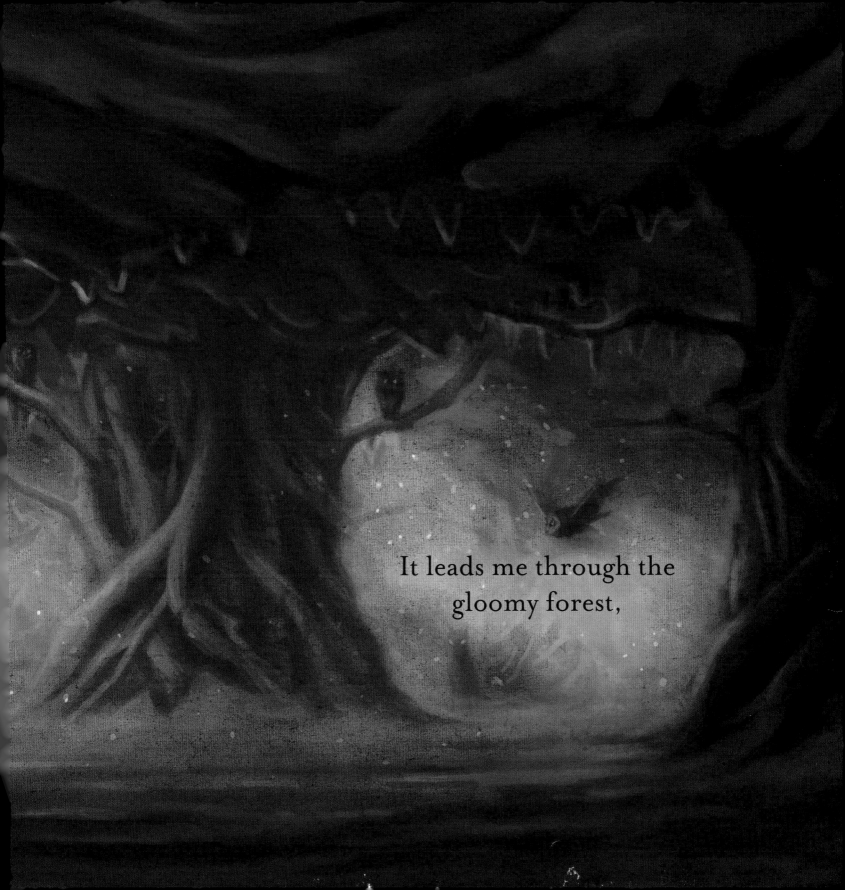

It leads me through the
gloomy forest,

where I meet the
Queen of the Poles.

She takes me to a secret place

with tiny fairies that glow.

I see thousands
of elves

and other
magical creatures.

And I can go there
every day...

because my favorite book
takes me there.

THE END

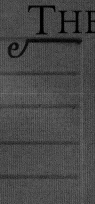

A FEIWEL AND FRIENDS BOOK
An Imprint of Macmillan

WHEN IT SNOWS. Copyright © 2012 by Richard Collingridge.
All rights reserved. Printed in China by Toppan Leefung Printing Ltd., Dongguan City, Guangdong
Province. For information, address Feiwel and Friends, 175 Fifth Avenue, New York, N.Y. 10010.
A CIP catalogue record for this book is available.
Originally published in Great Britain by David Fickling Books, a division of Random House
Children's Books. First published in the U.S. by Feiwel and Friends, an imprint of Macmillan.
ISBN: 978-1-250-02831-0
Feiwel and Friends logo designed by Filomena Tuosto
First U.S. Edition 2013
1 3 5 7 9 10 8 6 4 2
mackids.com

To Kim and Françoise